The Winter Hedgehog

A RED FOX BOOK: 0 09 980940 0

First published in Great Britain by Hutchinson
An imprint of Random House Children's Books

Hutchinson edition published 1989

1 3 5 7 9 10 8 6 4 2

Text © Ann Cartwright 1989
Illustrations © Reg Cartwright 1989

The right of Ann and Reg Cartwright
to be identified as the author and illustrator of this work
has been asserted in accordance with the
Copyright, Designs and Patents Act 1988

RANDOM HOUSE CHILDREN'S BOOKS
61–63 Uxbridge Rd, London W5 5SA
A division of The Random House Group Ltd

RANDOM HOUSE AUSTRALIA (PTY) LTD
20 Alfred Street, Milsons Point, Sydney,
New South Wales 2061, Australia

RANDOM HOUSE NEW ZEALAND LTD
18 Poland Road, Glenfield, Auckland 10, New Zealand

RANDOM HOUSE (PTY) LTD
Endulini, 5A Jubilee Road, Parktown 2193, South Africa

THE RANDOM HOUSE GROUP Limited Reg. No. 954009
www.randomhouse.co.uk

A CIP catalogue record for this book is available from the British Library.

Printed in Hong Kong

The Winter Hedgehog

ANN & REG CARTWRIGHT

RED FOX

ONE cold, misty autumn afternoon, the
hedgehogs gathered in a wood. They
were searching the undergrowth for
leaves for their nests, preparing for the long sleep
of winter.

All that is, except one.

The smallest hedgehog had overheard two
foxes talking about winter. 'What is winter?' he
had asked his mother.

'Winter comes when we are asleep,' she had
replied. 'It can be beautiful, but it can also be
dangerous, cruel and very, very cold. It's not for
the likes of us. Now go to sleep.'

But the smallest hedgehog couldn't sleep. As evening fell he slipped away to look for winter. When hedgehogs are determined they can move very swiftly, and soon the little hedgehog was far from home. An owl swooped down from high in a tree.

'Hurry home,' he called. 'It's time for your long sleep.' But on and on went the smallest hedgehog until the sky turned dark and the trees were nothing but shadows.

The next morning, the hedgehog awoke to find
the countryside covered in fog. 'Who goes
there?' called a voice, and a large rabbit emerged
from the mist; amazed to see a hedgehog about
with winter coming on.

'I'm looking for winter,' replied the hedgehog.
'Can you tell me where it is?'

'Hurry home,' said the rabbit. 'Winter is on
its way and it's no time for hedgehogs.'

But the smallest hedgehog wouldn't listen.
He was determined to find winter.

Days passed. The little hedgehog found plenty of slugs and insects to eat, but he couldn't find winter anywhere.

Then one day the air turned icy cold. Birds flew home to their roosts and the animals hid in their burrows and warrens. The smallest hedgehog felt very lonely and afraid and wished he was asleep with the other hedgehogs. But it was too late to turn back now!

That night winter came. A frosty wind swept
through the grass and blew the last straggling
leaves from the trees. In the morning the whole
countryside was covered in a carpet of snow.

'Winter!' cried the smallest hedgehog. 'I've
found it at last.' And all the birds flew down
from the trees to join him.

The trees were completely bare and the snow sparkled on the grass. The little hedgehog went to the river to drink, but it was frozen. He shivered, shook his prickles and stepped on to the ice. His feet began to slide and the faster he scurried, the faster he sped across it. 'Winter is wonderful,' he cried. At first he did not see the fox, like a dark shadow, slinking towards him.

'Hello! Come and join me,' he called as the fox reached the riverbank. But the fox only heard the rumble of his empty belly. With one leap he pounced on to the ice. When the little hedgehog saw his sly yellow eyes he understood what the fox was about. But every time he tried to run away he slipped on the ice. He curled into a ball and spiked his prickles.

'Ouch!' cried the fox. The sharp prickles stabbed his paws and he reeled towards the centre of the river where he disappeared beneath the thin ice.

'That was close,' the smallest hedgehog cried to himself. 'Winter is beautiful, but it is also cruel, dangerous and very, very cold.'

Winter was everywhere: in the air, in the trees, on the ground and in the hedgerows. Colder and colder it grew until the snow froze under the hedgehog's feet. Then the snow came again and a cruel north wind picked it up and whipped it into a blizzard. The night fell as black as ink and he lost his way. 'Winter is dangerous and cruel and very, very cold,' moaned the little hedgehog.

Luck saved him. A hare scurrying home gave him shelter in his burrow. By morning the snow was still falling, but gently now, covering everything it touched in a soft white blanket.

The smallest hedgehog was enchanted as he
watched the pattern his paws made. Reaching
the top of a hill, he rolled into a ball and
spun over and over, turning himself into a great
white snowball as he went. Down and down he
rolled until he reached the feet of two children
building a snowman.

'Hey, look at this,' said the little girl; 'a perfect
head for our snowman.'

'I'm a hedgehog,' he cried. But no one heard his tiny hedgehog voice.

The girl placed the hedgehog snowball on the snowman's body and the boy used a carrot for a nose and pebbles for the eyes. 'Let me out,' shouted the hedgehog. But the children just stood back and admired their work before going home for lunch.

When the children had gone, the cold and hungry hedgehog nibbled at the carrot nose. As he munched the sun came out and the snow began to melt. He blinked in the bright sunlight, tumbled down the snowman's body and was free.

Time went on. The hedgehog saw the world in
its winter cloak. He saw bright red berries
disappear from the hedgerows as the birds
collected them for their winter larders. And he
watched children speed down the hill on their
sleighs.

   The winter passed. One day the air grew
warmer and the river began to flow again. A
stoat, who had changed his coat to winter
white, changed it back to brown. Then
the little hedgehog found crocuses and
snowdrops beneath the trees and he knew it
was time to go home. Slowly he made his way
back to the wood.

From out of every log, sleepy hedgehogs were emerging from their long sleep.

'Where have you been?' they called to the smallest hedgehog.

'I found winter,' he replied.

'And what was it like?' asked his mother.

'It was wonderful and beautiful, but it was also....'

'Dangerous, cruel and very, very cold,' finished his mother.

But she was answered by a yawn, a sigh and a snore and the smallest hedgehog was fast asleep.

More Red Fox picture books
for you to enjoy

ELMER
by David McKee 0099697203

MUMMY LAID AN EGG
by Babette Cole 0099299119

RUNAWAY TRAIN
by Benedict Blathwayt 0099385716

DOGGER
by Shirley Hughes 009992790X

WHERE THE WILD THINGS ARE
by Maurice Sendak 0099408392

OLD BEAR
by Jane Hissey 0099265761

MISTER MAGNOLIA
by Quentin Blake 0099400421

ALFIE GETS IN FIRST
by Shirley Hughes 0099855607

OI! GET OFF OUR TRAIN
by John Burningham 009985340X

GORGEOUS
by Caroline Castle and Sam Childs 0099400766